This book belongs to

Aileen

DISNEY PRINCESS

VOLUME II

A READ-ALOUD STORYBOOK COLLECTION

Adapted by Frank Berrios

Illustrated by the Disney Storybook Artists

Random House 🏠 New York

Copyright © 2004 Disney Enterprises, Inc. All rights reserved under International and Pan-American Copyright Conventions. Published in the United States by Random House Children's Books, a division of Random House, Inc., New York, and simultaneously in Canada by Random House of Canada Limited, Toronto, in conjunction with Disney Enterprises, Inc. RANDOM HOUSE and the Random House colophon are registered trademarks of Random House, Inc. Some of the illustrations were originally published in *Beauty and the Beast: A Read-Aloud Storybook,* by Random House, Inc., in 1999 and in *The Little Mermaid: A Read-Aloud Storybook,* by Random House, Inc., in 2000. www.randomhouse.com/kids/disney

Library of Congress Control Number: 2003110532
ISBN: 0-7364-2241-2

Printed in the United States of America
10 9 8 7 6 5 4 3

Beauty and the Beast

One cold winter's evening, a beggar offered a prince a red rose in return for shelter in his castle. The Prince laughed at the gift and turned her away—only to find out that the beggar was really an enchantress!

The Enchantress turned the Prince into a hideous beast and put a spell on everyone in the castle. She left behind only the rose she had offered him. For the spell to be broken, the Prince would have to love another—and earn that person's love in return—before the rose's last petal fell.

Not far from the castle, a beautiful young woman named Belle lived with her father. She loved to read books about adventure and romance.

When Gaston the hunter saw Belle, he boasted, "That's the girl I'm going to marry."

One day, Belle's father, Maurice, set off for a fair.
He soon became lost in the dark, scary forest.

After being chased by a pack of hungry wolves, Maurice found himself at the gates of a mysterious castle. He forced the gates open and escaped from the wolves just in time!

Once inside, Belle's father was surprised to learn that this was no ordinary castle. All the servants had been changed into enchanted objects. And even worse, their master was a horrible beast!

When her father's horse, Phillipe, returned home alone, Belle knew something was wrong. So she rode Phillipe until he brought her to the spooky castle.

Belle entered the castle and discovered that her father was being held prisoner. Before she could free him, she heard someone approaching.

It was the Beast! Belle begged him to release her father, but the Beast refused. "Wait!" said Belle. "Take me instead!" The Beast agreed, and Belle's father was set free.

Soon Belle became friends with Mrs. Potts, Chip, and the other living objects in the castle. The Beast allowed Belle to go anywhere in the castle—except for the West Wing.

But one day, Belle's curiosity got the better of her. She entered the West Wing and discovered the enchanted rose. When the Beast found her, he was so furious that he ordered Belle to leave the castle.

As Belle rode away from the castle, she was quickly surrounded by a pack of snarling wolves. Just as they were about to attack, the Beast appeared.

A wolf bit the Beast on his arm and he threw the wolf against a tree. The rest of the pack attacked him, but he chased them away. The Beast had saved Belle!

Back at the castle, Belle tended to the Beast's wound. As the days passed, Belle realized that the Beast was actually very gentle and sweet. One night they shared a dance! Belle was becoming very fond of the Beast.

The Beast asked Belle if she was happy.

"Yes," answered Belle, "if only I could see my father again." So the Beast brought her a magic mirror. Belle saw Maurice—lost and alone in the woods, looking for her! The Beast told Belle to leave the castle and help her father.

Belle found her father and brought him safely home. But before she could return to the castle, Gaston arrived with an angry crowd.

Some of the villagers had heard about the Beast. Gaston convinced them to go to the castle and destroy the monster!

When Gaston and the villagers entered the castle, everything was quiet. Suddenly, Lumiere, the candelabrum, yelled, "Now!"—and the mob was ambushed by an army of enchanted dishes and furniture! Spoons flew through the air as pots and pans rained down on the unsuspecting villagers.

Gaston escaped and searched the entire castle until he found the Beast. Gaston fired an arrow—but the Beast didn't fight back. Without Belle, he had lost the will to live.

Just then, Belle returned, and the Beast felt his sad heart fill with love again! He leaped to his feet and grabbed Gaston.

When the cowardly hunter begged for mercy, the Beast let him go. But as the Beast turned around, Gaston stabbed him in the back! The Beast let out a mighty roar, and Gaston tripped and fell off the balcony. Belle began to cry as the Beast lay on the ground.

"I love you," she said—and with those words, the Beast was magically transformed into the prince he had once been. The spell was broken!

Joyfully, Mrs. Potts, Chip, Lumiere, and all the enchanted objects in the castle returned to human form. And Belle and the Prince lived happily ever after!

The Little Mermaid

All the creatures of the sea had gathered for Sebastian's royal concert in honor of King Triton. Triton's daughters were going to sing—but one was missing!

"Ariel!" cried King Triton.

Princess Ariel had forgotten all about the concert. She was busy exploring a sunken ship with her friend Flounder. Ariel loved to collect things from the human world above the sea.

Ariel and Flounder brought one of their treasures to Scuttle the seagull. He taught Ariel everything he knew about the human world.

"This is a dinglehopper," explained Scuttle. "Humans use these to straighten their hair."

Later that day, Ariel decided to go human-watching near a big ship. A handsome young prince named Eric caught her eye—it was love at first sight!

Suddenly, a storm began to rage. Hurricane winds howled and giant waves tossed the ship onto some jagged rocks. Prince Eric was thrown into the sea! Ariel knew she had to save him.

Ariel used all her strength to pull Prince Eric safely to shore. She started to sing a beautiful song to the prince. As he began to awaken, Ariel slipped into the sea and swam home, heartbroken.

When King Triton learned that Ariel had been to the surface, he became furious! The king destroyed Ariel's collection of human objects and ordered her never to go near humans again.

Ariel was very sad. So she went to the sea witch, Ursula, for help. Ursula promised to turn Ariel into a human—in exchange for her voice! Ariel agreed, and using her evil magic, the sea witch took Ariel's voice and trapped it in a seashell locket.

Suddenly, Ariel's tail turned into legs. The spell worked—but there was a catch! If the prince didn't fall in love with Ariel in three days, she would turn back into a mermaid and belong to Ursula forever!

Ariel found her handsome prince. But without her voice, the princess couldn't sing to Eric or tell him who she was. Although he didn't know that Ariel was the one who had saved him, Prince Eric grew to like her very much.

But Ursula wouldn't let Ariel win Prince Eric's heart so easily! She used her magic to turn herself into a pretty girl named Vanessa...

. . . and used Ariel's voice from the locket to put the prince under her spell!

The next morning, Ariel learned that Prince Eric and Vanessa were to be married that very day! But Scuttle soon discovered that Vanessa was actually Ursula in disguise.

"Find a way to stall that wedding!" yelled Sebastian the crab, as Scuttle flew off toward the wedding on the boat. Ariel had to hurry—there wasn't much time left!

Scuttle and his friends did what they could to stop
the wedding.

"Why, you little . . . ," screamed Vanessa. Just
then, Scuttle tore the seashell locket from her neck.

Vanessa's seashell locket shattered just as Ariel reached the ship. Ariel had her voice back! Once Prince Eric heard her speak, he realized he had been tricked.

"You're too late!" shrieked Ursula as she returned to her true form. Ariel looked down in shock to see that her legs had turned back into a mermaid's tail!

Ursula grabbed Ariel and dove into the sea. Suddenly,
King Triton appeared!

The sea witch told Triton about the deal she had made with Ariel. In exchange for his daughter's freedom, the king agreed to take Ariel's place.

"Now I am ruler of all the ocean!" shouted Ursula. She used her powers to grow to a monstrous size. But brave Prince Eric would not be defeated. He drove his ship right into Ursula and destroyed the evil sea witch!

King Triton was free! And although he knew he would miss her greatly, the king granted Ariel's wish and changed her back into a human.

All the sea creatures gathered to see Prince Eric and Ariel get married. The new couple sailed away and lived happily ever after.

Aladdin

One morning in a faraway palace in Agrabah, the Sultan was arguing with his daughter, Princess Jasmine. "The law says you must be married to a prince by your next birthday," he said. "And that's only three days away!"

But the princess had other ideas. "When I marry, I want it to be for love," she said.

That night, Princess Jasmine decided to run away. "I don't want to be a princess anymore," she said. But Rajah, her pet tiger, tried to stop her. "I'm sorry, Rajah," said Jasmine. "I can't stay here and have my life lived for me." Then she climbed over the palace wall.

The princess found herself in the busy marketplace. She took an apple from a cart and gave it to a hungry child. The fruit seller asked Jasmine to pay for it, but she had no money.

Suddenly, a handsome young man named Aladdin appeared. He tried to convince the fruit seller that Jasmine was not a thief. But soon they were both being chased by the palace guards!

Aladdin took Jasmine to his secret rooftop home.
He was falling in love with the beautiful young
woman. Just as they were about to kiss, the palace
guards stormed up and grabbed Aladdin!

Princess Jasmine threw back her hood and ordered the palace guards to release Aladdin. The guards were surprised to see the princess outside the palace, but they told her that Jafar, the Sultan's advisor, had sent them to find Aladdin. So Princess Jasmine hurried back to the castle.

53

"Why do you want that young man from the marketplace?" Jasmine asked Jafar.

"The boy was a criminal," said Jafar. "Sadly, his sentence has already been carried out—death."

"How could you?" cried Jasmine, heartbroken.

Not long after, a prince named Ali made a grand entrance into the Sultan's throne room. "I have journeyed from afar to seek your daughter's hand in marriage."

But Princess Jasmine was not impressed with the prince and ran off.

That night, Prince Ali visited Jasmine in her room and took her for a ride on his Magic Carpet. Soon Jasmine realized that Prince Ali was actually the young man from the marketplace. Jasmine was happy to learn that he was still alive—but she didn't know that Aladdin wasn't really a prince. Aladdin had found a magic lamp with a genie inside, and the Genie had turned him into a prince!

By the end of the night, Jasmine had fallen in love.
She would choose to marry Aladdin!

But Jafar had other plans! He wanted to marry the princess himself so that he could become Sultan. So Jafar stole the magic lamp from Aladdin. The Genie had to grant Jafar three wishes!

Jafar's first wish was to be Sultan. His second wish was to become the most powerful sorcerer in the world. Aladdin watched in horror as Jafar enslaved Princess Jasmine and the Sultan. Then the villain used his evil magic to transform himself into a giant cobra!

Aladdin had to save Jasmine! He knew he couldn't defeat Jafar's magic, but he had one last trick up his sleeve. "The Genie has more power than you'll ever have," Aladdin taunted. "Face it, Jafar, you're still just second best."

So with his third wish, the power-hungry Jafar asked to become a genie!

But what Jafar didn't realize was that every genie is imprisoned in a lamp. The evil villain was trapped by his own wish. Aladdin had saved the princess and the Sultan!

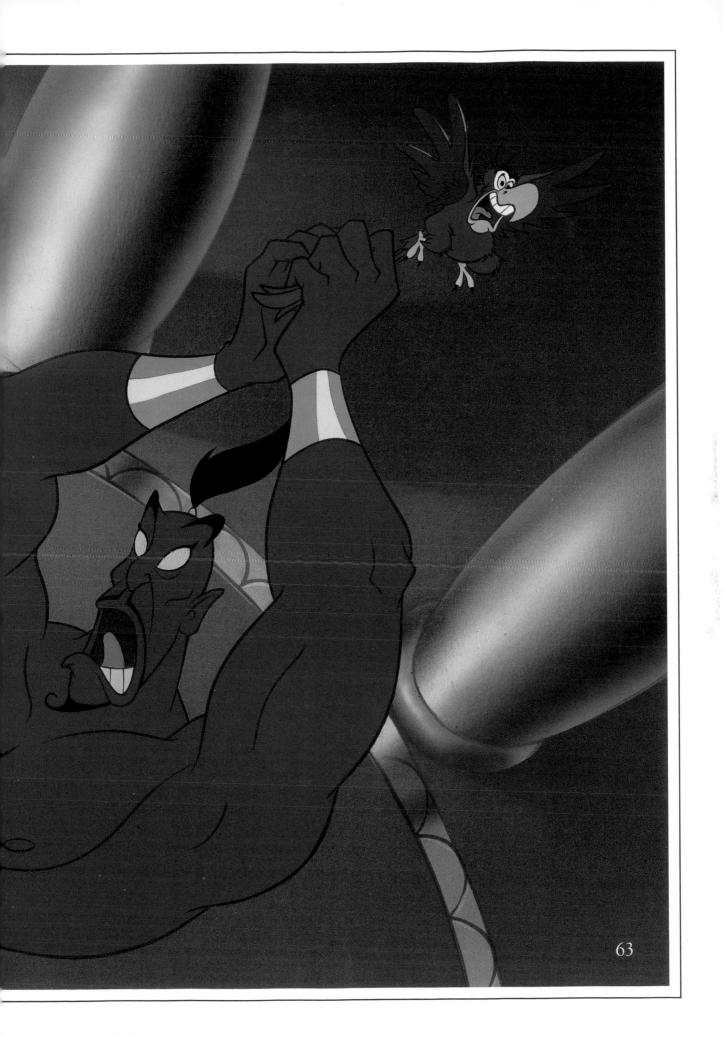

The Sultan announced that Princess Jasmine could marry anyone she thought was worthy. She chose Aladdin! And together they lived happily ever after.

KERRY 2 ALYD